The
Luminol
Reels

Laura Ellen Joyce

THE LUMINOL REELS

ISBN 978-1-940853-04-8

designed by Cal A. Mari

published by Calamari Press
NY, NY

www.calamaripress.com

For Cassie and Kate.

AGONIES

Mothering

The autopsy reel is always brutal.

Y-Incision

There are requisite smells, leaks and metallics. There is no end to this reel. The murderers can program it for severity.

It begins in the intimacy of the cubicle. The doctor's fleshy hands will draw back the sheet just far enough to see the Y-incision. You will remember the nine months the baby swam through your stomachache black sea.

The doctor has one glass eye and the other dilates obscenely at the carnage.

Dollflesh

This one comes next. A close-up of her clean dollflesh. It is sewn up but there is a special effect— it blazes. The effect is of a hostile sun; a bloody light looms from inside. Cut back to her treacly hair scraped back. The braids you twisted in have been displaced. Blood on her lips. Her eyes have a cloudy look, filmed with something white and viscous. End.

Ghost Town

Whether you can see this reel or not will give you the first clue.

Don't expect there to be any respite if you are dead. The only privileges of the dead are unregulated menstruation and fewer night shifts.

She has walked across the desert at the most dangerous times—during luminol crashes; after swallowing cardiac spores. She wears Kylie hotpants and has Marilyn hair. The first time she is raped there is a splash of red across the sand.

She has a xanax smile as she walks on glass slippers, as she glides through the burning sand in figure eights.

The next scene she is holding a package, a birthday gift in gold paper. Confetti bursts from her mouth as she opens the box.

The final scene is overexposed. The desert has an alpine look. Her fall is heavily accented with extra-diegetic sounds: a breach birth, a violin concerto written by a fascist, mouth fucking and dilated pupils are recorded in layers.

Holy Water

This reel should be handled with care. Once dried out it has no further effect.

Play this reel only in dire circumstances. Cardiac spores should not be concurrent and are not to be swallowed at this time. The water is thick with luminol and should not be entered naked. Any last desires will be played on this reel.

Stars

When you eat the stars there will be a psychosis.

Stars are to be used with the following reels: Big Dipper, Oracle.

BIG DIPPER

You become too tired to get up and oil the Big Dipper, too weary to bring raw fish to the bears and at first you will lie under the heavy weight of sleep with no reprieve. When you begin to flitter through wakefulness, it is brutal. You will have a low-grade humming comedown and there is no way to fend it off—not ten years sleep, not one hundred years could numb it.

There should be a glass of water, frosted crystal, five cubes of ice, a gentle fizz. In an enamel pillbox lies a handful of stars, speckled duck-egg blue. You feel slightly sicker; a groaning will go through you, and a slam of pain. A shivering—a bad, hot shivering—is next.

Sleeplessness is better; take the soft blue pellets on cracked tongues and sip—like invalids—at the icy drinks. And then it will come, oh virgin, will come again, more intense. You will be dizzy, crawling on the bed, reaching sallow hands out of the window to feel the lick of air. You moan loud, grouching at the itchy fever on the edge ... peeling away from your high.

ORACLE

The virgin appears. She will fall through the glass at your feet, comes with green fire at your throat. You will talk neon bullshit for hours ... or maybe for one minute. The virgin gives you water which you will crave beyond belief.

You will see her, more beautiful than the crucified Jesus. She offers you death–a slow drugless bludgeoning of horror. Finally, you open your eyes on her dirt bed. The mossy cold will be so good on your skin. You feel your mouth break wide open to smile a crazy water balloon of joy.

Fingerlube

They applied fingerlube before the sweet sixteen reel.

We stood in a line while every opening and yaw was sharpied in rainbow colours.

We were scared of the reel; no one knew exactly what was to come. They applied strong glue below the nostrils, a hit per breath—clocks of fright gleamed upwards, back into the brain, a cold fug releasing there. Slime was brought in from the splash show, a bucket each of custard yellow clouded out the eyes. Heavy dairy lay on our vision, while below a rawness ached. Slammed outwards, y-shaped, our mermaid openings began to empty of scales.

Factory

This reel is educational and must be broadcast during the entirety of Fur.

This reel is on a loop. It contains vintage footage of the master butcher. She guides you through the factory tasks.

First, she tells you where materials can be sourced: from the enclosure between the animal pens. She tells you the shape the materials will be in: Some of them may be alive and ranting, some will be unconscious and some plain dead. There may occasionally be only body parts, that have been gnawed on. She tells you the first part of the task: sift through the girls in the cage (once they are tied up) and take a sack to collect any odds and ends.

The next part of the reel shows the workroom and the chemicals you will need for the job. The workroom is full of barrels and creels and jars. There you will find acids and oils that strip flesh right off the bone.

The master butcher gives some advice at this point: The first time you touch a girl you might vomit or get the shakes. She reminds you to think of how exquisite it is to saw a girl in half without spilling a drop of blood. She claims that one day you can be as talented as her. This is false encouragement. Since her martyrdom there has been no one to take her place.

Finally she shows you how she does it, in real time. First she gets rid of the blood by hanging the girl upside down and slitting her throat. Then she sews the girl back up. The liquids collect in a glass tank. They layer down—watery red, yellow fat, with shiny white gobs of plasmic waste. In the centre blooms a starburst of hot red—the richest blood fresh from her heart. It pulses and steams, lazy drifts staining the fat, the plasma, the pinkish water. She stirs the mixture carefully, for hours, until the heart blood atomises and spreads its magic through the gloop.

When it is time for the show she brings the girl out on stage. The effect is breathtaking.

Quinceañera

This reel does not require fingerlube, but a quantity of dental dams should be distributed.

The howling of wolves can first be sweetened in a tin can and then piped through the room.

Once the reel is lit, the splatter can be arranged in abstract blurs. Girls should be dropped suddenly against a wall, using a limbless drag to spread the blood. Use two vials of luminol and shake it out until the blue-glow scatters—astral—in the dormitory.

The dead girls should then be removed, the beds pushed back against the wall.

Your dresses will breathe into your ears, their wrinkles hushed like velvet.

Bad moon songs rise all night and you will burst grand mal through the sparkle, flatlining before dawn.

Badlands

This should only be used when playing dead.

This is imported footage of a multiple cadaver show.

We were caught in the centre of the desert when this reel started. The sky crashed out into luminol before we had a chance to shelter.

We saw the twins playing dead and we ran. It felt like the end.

The juice of the sky dripped down and vanished. In ten minutes flat we were in the blue dark and the sand was loose and our feet were wet. We slipped into a hole and the twins pulled us down. Our teeth chattered and our breathing wasn't right.

There was the sound of a dog. Yap yap yap yap. A boot to our faces and then soft, slick fingers along our throats. One of us screamed. And the blood from the sky stained our insides blue.

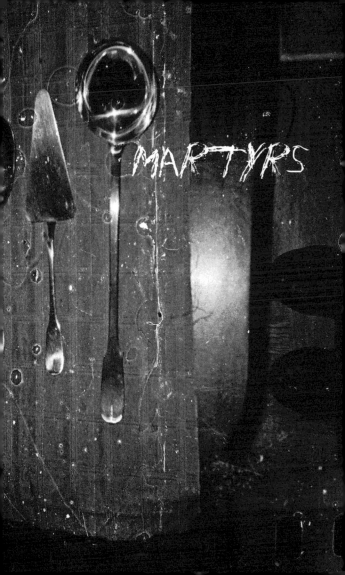

Candyfloss

Patron of Innocence, Pageants, Virginity.

This reel must be played only at dawn and twilight. It may accompany the deaths of children; vigils and funerals if there has been no sexual contact (forced or natural). Or at any séance where two or more gods are invoked.

It may never be used pornographically or for vaginal pleasure.

Nudist

Patron of Interstitiality, Reversals, Surgeries.

Do not attempt this at sundown. There is no return once started. You will be under the knife immediately. If there is suspicion of an interstitial pregnancy, this reel can help to flush it out.

If there is a birth and you need to reverse the child, this is the best way to do it.

Party Queen

Patron of Partying, Soft Deaths, Visions.

This can be applied to imprisoned, hospitalised or housebound women. Never take full stars with this, though a luminol rag is to be encouraged. Likewise, heavy dairy or cold glue can be used.

This reel is on a soft loop—each time it will fade until coma is achieved.

Mechanic

Patron of Explosions, Thrills, Disasters.

Nails into the palms must precede this reel, which can be programmed for intervals.

The intervals are as follows: grease the tracks with lard, fuel the big dipper with red diesel, sit in the rickety cars and fly beltless around sharp bends.

Witch

Patron of Secrets, Cannibalism, Plastic.

Dismemberment and Mutilation reel.

First sharpen all knives. Dip each hand, wrist-deep, into luminol.

The reel begins at the moment of unwrapping. The long knife is used to slice the cellophane. Fragments of pink peignoir still cling to the witch's flesh and there is blood at the corner of her mouth. The story of the waterfall will begin. The witch looks fragile, as her peppermint teeth stick out and the peignoir falls away.

MURDERERS

Coat Hanger

This may be used when a girl gives false urine for her daily sample.

The reel starts with the girl. She is wearing Jackie O sunglasses and running in the clogged sand, the sun in her face. She looks sick, worried that we are half-serious. She doesn't stop but keeps swigging from her 12oz cherry wine. The neck of the bottle is sticky and reddish gobs of liquid dribble over the sides.

We feel exhilarated, thrilled by this girl with a scarf in her hair and green eyes. When we crept up she had been lying on her front, bare feet tracing the sand, singing a sad song, wailing across the blue dirt. When we begin to abuse her (under our breath) she gets to her feet and starts running, never losing hold of the wine.

The girl with green eyes looks so defiant she is radiant. She swallows the last drops of sweet wine, wipes her mouth with the back of her hand and drops the glass bottle on the sand where it smashes. We stop circling. We hold back on the horses then. We whisper to the girl that we will cut her into tiny pieces. The girl lights a cigarette and sits cross-legged looking into the blue distance. Then she starts shouting. You are liars, baby, rotten dirty liars.

We feel a jolt through us. We know these kinds of girls so well. With their cherry wine and cigarettes, their transistor radios tuned to the oldies, Blue Velvet pouring through them, as they imagined the supreme thrill of a bad man—a bad man who might kill one of them. Wriggling closer under the patchwork quilts their dead mothers had made in sanatoria or asylums. But now there is no bad man, there is only us. We kneel beside her and put our hands dusted with blue sand on the girl's abdomen. Our mouths are dry. There is no sound but the breathing of the girl. We dare not exhale.

Her plumpness is not just puppy fat. The green-eyed girl is in a daze—she seemed to forget that there is no way she is leaving alive. She stands up unsteadily, singing Blue Velvet and swaying. We watch her go a little way. She takes her shoes off and empties the sand on to the ground. As she bends forwards, she stumbles and sits down.

We put our fingers on her throat. We wrap a blindfold around her eyes, gently pulling her hair free of its ponytail. The coathanger is engaged.

Bluebeard

This Daddy Reel can be used for psychological terror.

The zone is the old apartment. You are shown the bed where you were conceived. The chaos that flew between your parents when they fucked has soiled the mattress now flaked with rot. Bugs grow fat and jumpy in the gaping whorls that pock its surface—a dead zone teeming with riotous filth.

The door is thrown open and sunlight is let in. The itchy mattress collapses into dust and nothing remains but an old iron bedstead. You have brought armfuls of lilies with you and two tons of dark mulch. As you pack the bedstead with the dark earth and decorate it with flowers, you sense your own grave. You cannot breathe.

There is a slow lag of time ... darkness falls. It is midnight—the time flashes on the reel. You can hear laughter leaking though the door of the apartment.

The reel skips and now you are lying flat on your back. Lilies crowd your feet. Two stars are tattooed on your face like fat tears. Coiled snakes blacken her hair and poison bubbles in her ears so you cannot hear your heartbeats.

There is a suitcase beside the bed, limbs neatly packed inside. A red rope hangs above you, made of fingernails and hair, the knife swinging close. Your thorax is closed, puckered with scars from your blood weddings.

The blood on your fingers smells fresh and cinnamony. Sharper is the scent of bleach used on the fleshless legs in the suitcase. There are scraps of puce skin and yellow fat adhering to the bone— these six legs had been dumped in vats of domestic product.

The heat seeps into the boards until they are swollen tight, their colour leaching white in the sun. The air is sodden and heavy. Fat salty drops scald your tongue.

Child Killer

This is a gory transparency, backlit by luminol.

The first time a friendship ring was found here, it was crushed, trampled. The blue heart stone— set in its transparency—fluttered in plastic like a flickering shutter, a reel.

A man sleeps, soft as a foetus, curled around his axe. The blade is glued with kisses, semen crackling yellow down its length. There is a violent ceremony where he marries the knife. The blood in his dream is visible—endless, sweet and warm. The honeymoon becomes obscene, blackout, fade.

His dreams are havoc. He had no control. He could not hide his passion for the axe and the knife. He could not make his loves make sense.

We laugh at him but cannot hear our own voices. We giggle as though we are children hell-bent on letting the adults know we understand their filthy jokes.

The damp patch on her skin, hair like sugar, like sin.
The flush of scarlet on her flesh. Six silver buttons
on her dress, I saw them shining in the dirt. Oh you
could be so careless.

This song is to appease or anger the child killer. Before the factory, before the pageants, before the dead girls, there was nothing here—just white sand and silence. Girls walked into the desert, in pairs and groups. They brought their radios and guitars and patchwork quilts. They brought marijuana and acid stars and cherry wine.

Then there was another discovery—slides that had been partially burned but still showed a child playing hopscotch, her treacle hair dancing in loops. There were just a few ribbons left—dry, filmy ends. The last scene is cut, the girl is pulled down from the piñon tree, her silver shoes falling through the air.

Now she is trapped in glass and dances in the projector. There is a shrine for her in the virgin's grotto. Pinecones spray-painted silver are left beside it to make the nights festive.

Flesh

During the Flesh reel you see the baby crawling from your womb. You will see it half-dead, dragging through the muck at your feet, shards of glass pricking its soft mouth and screams, screams, screams. You must sit still and watch the shows; women with surgery lips roiled naked on yachts, scraps of metallic fabric stretched taut over nipples and pubic mounds. There are often two masked men shouting abuse in filthy streams and putting their big hands all over. Laddered scars creep up from the women's bellies. Close-up shots show smeared makeup gathering in patches beneath their breasts. Redness and sores creep from their cracked nipples where men yank the fabric free. The baby will see too but she won't understand.

When the show ends, take your shucking knife and cut a line in red right down the pubic bone. Your fingers will plunge inside—you'll draw the flaps of skin wide open, ten metal staples closing up the wound.

Daddy

We ran miles of forest every night from daddy. We pricked our skin and scored it with sugar and paprika. We smothered our hair in cocoa butter and stuffed cloves in our dark vaginas. We drank vinegar with our bath in the evening, to vomit anything in our food. We were plump and pretty, our skin glowed like a Chinese lantern and he wanted our laughter for himself.

The first time he caught us we all held our breath waiting to see what he would do. We felt the red haze of blood smashing through our weaker hearts, pains in our chest as we ran until exhausted, our sleek muscles coiled shut. We flew forward on our hands and tipped ourselves into the shallows of the lake to soothe the blaze in our aching legs.

We laughed ourselves sick on the big dipper, our frazzled heartbeats pumping acid round. We lay, gleaming, toads running along our padded toes, sucking out the thorns with bleeding mouths.

He buried his pretty thing, his axe, beneath the rotten leaves. We did not say a word but laughed cleanly, no black bile spraying out, no pus running down our chins. He was amazed at our health, we looked perfect. My pretty, pretty thing, he said again and plunged his hands into the red dirt and scooped out some worthless trash—diamonds, veiny eggshells smeared with afterbirth and dead daisies. He made them into crowns and placed the trophies on our heads.

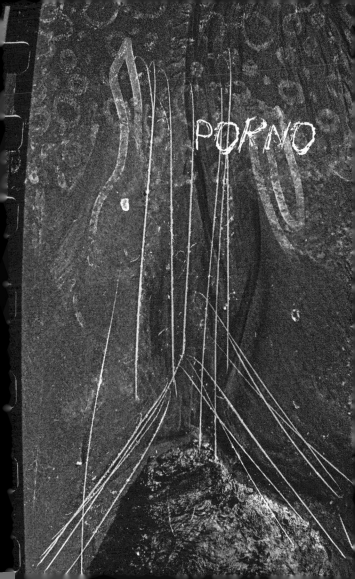

Sugar

As she put her tiny hand in his, red diesel stained his palm.

He brought her a stick of candyfloss; it frothed around her face, sugar crystals caught between milk teeth as he put his hands around her neck.

Behind the generators and the waste disposal units, a white puddle ran down.

Girl on Girl

Nudity compelled the girl who minded the elephants. She took off her filthy clothes and lay down in the heat, a stink rising from her.

She tanned her small breasts, ironed flat, like all of ours, from birth.

Dirty girl, she wanted to see. She went to the dead place, where the candyfloss girl lay. She had a bucket of stunned fish, for the white bear. There was a slash of lightning, a burr of heat which struck the metal pail. The three fish jumped out of the water, grew molten and fell back down.

The nudist lost her heartbeat, her hair smoked and she fell on to our blonde sister for the last time.

Buzzed

This reel is psychedelic.

You begin in the bed, alone in the dormitory. You have a luminol rag in your mouth. There is a mirror on the ceiling and you see your eyebags, your puckered mouth, your asphalt skin.

You dream that you can get out of bed. You don't. You lie and party alone.

Beside you is a folder full of scraps of skin and pressed flowers and the hair of saints. A glass of iced water and a vial of luminol within reach.

Cut to the desert. It is in flames. A man is atop a narrow platform, sawing at his arm.

Hard rubies fall into your mouth shutting off your sound.

You pull yourself to pieces. In the background an axe scrapes against the metal, crashing like the ocean.

Napalm

This one is for the sickos.

Napalm, sulphur and asbestos storms hit in Electric.

She is naked, greasing the rides.

Slow, slow, slow motion.

Her tiny heart bikini is ripped open by the clouds. Nacreous grains spray out of every hole and gap and slit. She is cut in pieces, shredded by its weight. Her flesh becomes confetti on her bones.

Snuff

This reel starts with an accidental strangling.

She starts to turn blue, she is dying. Your hands are shaking. You see the axe behind you on the wall and bring it down. You kiss her on the forehead—she is sharp and sour and full of darkness. You are desire.

There is violet on the bed—the sheets running full of sticky gobs. You wrap her tight in plastic sheeting, you let the excess collect.

There is time that is blank. You are on her and you are guilty.

Later, you get dreamy. You slash her open and taste her. When she is in pieces, you hang her to cure. When she is nothing but bone and pearl, you set her on flat paddles in the oven.

The parcels of smoked meat are the best you've ever tasted.

Gynoshow

This is the last reel he sent you.
His hand feels cool on your sutures.

Hired assassins gleam at you with needles.
Their knives jolt into dullness.

They cover your flesh with folds of paper.

In the dollhouse.
You lie with angled limbs like rigor.

The reel slices to show your opening—born without
a hole. Instead you have a gathered ruche of skin
that peaks, like the tip of a Hokusai wave. You have
a shuttered gap, a hoarding.

There is no slit for shedding wastes and they fill you
up.

You take a shucking knife and slide it through the
crest. It is over quickly. A gush of fluids cleans out
of you and splatters gore.

Threads of red hair loop you shut. There is a tiny
hole, to avoid disease.

Black Mass

This is in real time. But in the depths.

Listen to all the instructions and do not flinch at the butcher's strange request.

If it is not her, it will be you. You must remember that when inside this reel.

Outside, the sky will have a black look, above the dead-eyed, shuttered night.

You will be better off inside.

On the altar there is a cloth, darkly stained, deeper than red.

The butcher wears a matching robe. She tells you it is the colour of mourning.

Set the girl down amongst the butcher's dainty offerings:

Plum heart, brown lung. Balletic half-pigs, their sides pierced dry.

The taste of filthy pennies fills your mouth as you bring down the cleaver, like a monstrance stiff with blood.

At this point, catch the bloody pearl.

Twins

If there are twins, they must be sutured with the assistance of this reel.

All twins will be blasted with freckles, bound by a widow's peak. Surgery can take place on their tenth birthday.

Once you are gowned, spray their cunts with white foam that smells like a custard of baby fat. Scrape it off so that the foam and the mess of hair comes away leaving raised sores on their prickly skins. Do not put your mouth near that. Go on, they will say, in a teasing voice, and not even that gently they will try to push you down towards that bare red place. If they do, you must lick and kiss and tongue. You must feel every bump as you flick over the flesh and think of each pore, bacteria—a yellowy jelly that might burst at any time—in your vulnerable mouth. Blackheads will scud their thighs where sweat collects; blue, dense. Put two thumbnails around the toxic place and let the poison flow away. Scrub the pore out with salt and lime.

Following the operation, keep them sticky with pig lard, soft on their scars, where the heads are fused. If you have an unsteady hand their circuitry will come loose; blue sparks will fizz along their stomachs, intestines, shoulders, where the cord wraps them tight. Phantom limbs will give them pain and they will not keep silent.

Bearbaiting

Bearbaiting begins in Gold. All participants must drink luminol margaritas.

You will awaken underneath a tree. The bear cub will be at your side, licking your face clean of dried blood, whimpering. You will sit up, see that you are in the shantytown on the other side of the desert. Your ribs will ache as though you had been dragged all the way there.

The gold flags of the province are tied to the branches of the tree, and every one of the adobe and corrugated metal shelters is painted in heaven metals.

The second stage is to eat the fruit. It will be shimmering gold, and a viscous syrup will pour out—sharp and salty, it will refresh your thirst. You will feel weightless and stand on your damaged limbs, ready to run at the mama bear, take your weapon out and kill her cold.

There will seem to be a wide pool, and beside it a patch of lush grass where bears lie in a naked tumble. You stare at their beauty and begin to touch them, suck the blue salt from their matted fur. Tears will roll down, the bears will put their big hands all over your back, stroking it, pummelling it, kissing you.

You will scream, you will vomit. It will all be horror—
the desert a black slick flooding your eyes. You
will see the edge of the desert, trails of blackened
bones, coyotes and carrion. Clouds of insects buzz
low, flanking you, sucking blood-fat.

Mass Burial

The smell is rotten in the desert. Putrefaction is scrambled in the heat. Some of the girls lie with their faces missing, brains leaking from the dead zone, but with their right arms or feet still covered in creamy flesh.

Relief can be gained by visiting the mass grave. Run your fingers through their hair and breathe in their sharp, violent scents. Lie on top of them, rolling your heavy body over theirs, catching blue-black hair in your teeth and tasting their sweet perspiration where it collects underneath the fester and damp of their corpses.

Stillbirth

The bearpits run the length of the plant. Beneath the factory and the ovens and the dormitories. Behind the stage. There are passages between the zones—passages that have been reinforced to carry domestic product, vats of acid, barrows full of girls. Along these passages are cages and bearpits. Creels of the fresh or near dead are stored there. Some for the cadaver shows, some for the bears.

The white baby bear cries for her lover, the nudist.

She birthed a baby before she died—a muted, hairless spod that the bear sings to and squeezes. The nudist's ashes have been scattered through the zone.

A luminol mass is held for her once a year.

Desert Run

A walk across the desert—in plastic heels, heart-shaped sunglasses, chewing gum, drinking cherry wine, wearing a sequined bustier—is a film cliché.

Sunglasses snapped, sequins scattered, wine syruping into blue sand, bustier torn and rusty—is a parable.

Decide on your option before the reel begins.

Parable:

The sand had been clean once; a virgin sheet of white, soft and clean as cocaine. But now, there was the factory. Now the sand was a glitter of blue.

There were stories about the desert—the parable of Old Jack, the parable of the Child Killer. But the girls still came. They came at midnight, they came early in the morning. They walked in bare feet carrying plastic grocery bags with their uniforms, food, rape alarms. Keys were splayed in their palms, knifed out. The buses did not come at night, nor in the early morning. The women came to the desert, walked over the bodies they found there, careful to avoid falling down into the mass graves, the limb-filled holes of the desert.

CLICHÉ:

The sky is black, the sand so clotted with human that it reflects nothing. There is no wind, no water. The only way to cross is to take metallic salts every forty paces.

To walk across the desert is to conquer fear.

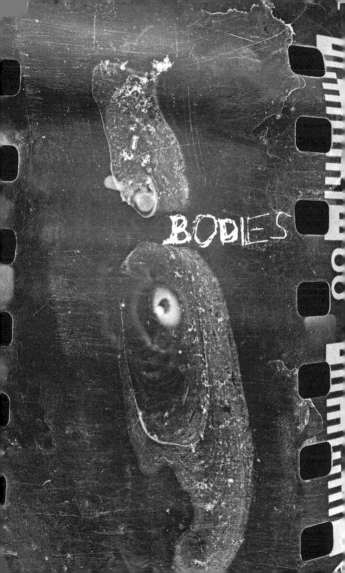

BODIES

Menstruation

BLACK:

Violently repeated with fatal consequences. Glass shards are used. Anxiety sickness is registered at one hundred decibels.

YELLOW:

Self-defence has been attempted and must be neutered. Offcuts and slough to be entered into the waste heap.

BLOOD:

Fucking is immaterial.

MILK:

Burned caramel runs along the length of the vulva. Licking is required; alternatively a longhandled spoon.

GENERAL:

Menstruation is regulated with pills. These are mandatory and administered via forced feeding. You will be strapped to the surgical chair and tubes will be inserted daily. The pills are safe and hygienic.

There will be pregnancy tests, smears and tissue scrapes done weekly. The resulting debris kept in glass jars. If there is any foetal matter this will be harboured separately.

Menstruation is encouraged in the dead girls. Their wombs are unregulated.

If there is any depression, breast tenderness or suicidal ideation present, this will be considered pre-menstrual and intervention will be severe.

Abortion

If there are remaining sisters, they can help remove the pregnancy.

They may bathe you as the pregnancy develops. They may paste wormwood onto your eyes and let you sleep for a full day or more, until the baby passes through you in hard pellets, wormy darts of flesh.

You may sit beneath the wormwood tree and cry, letting the green stink of it settle on your skin, pushing your softness against it. The dogs will moan all day. They will become so hungry that they start to eat each other. They sense the wormwood on your skin and stay away.

Fucking

Fuck in the cages. A Daddy reel can be programmed for severity.

SADISM REEL:

He will be scared of you when he makes the baby come. He will want you to stop. His legs shake when he smells you coming close. His sweat smells of vinegar. You will let him be daddy, guiding him gently at first, then, whoring him down in your black furze. He will cry and flinch at your fingers in his beard, your teeth on his tongue. You will meet in the tunnel that connects the cages and the dark spaces where the dead are stored.

ROMANCE REEL:

He will lay you down on the jewelled blanket from the cadaver show—gold, glittering, filthy with faeces and dirt from the floor. It is always ready for you, rolled behind creels of limbs and flesh. When he comes to meet you, he crawls through the tunnel, his knees smeared with fishguts. You wait on the rich-coloured rug, its gold tassels flecked with food and shit.

Baby Girl reel:

Your knickers will be white lace, to match your knee socks and training bra. They stink of cloves and vinegar, dribbled with patches of sticky brown molasses. You will remove all traces of hair.

Third Trimester reel:

Your breasts will be heavy, sweat dripping through your shirt like mustard. Let the hair grow thick on your pubic bone, the knotty curls clinging to the flesh of your thighs.

Pregnancy

This will be the worst time. You will be alone.

Your last remaining sisters will be feverish in the dormitory. You have to feed them from a tube of egg, from the dried food store. Plunge it deep into their mouths so they have to eat. They'll be happy to do it, they won't say no.

There will only be a few minutes of darkness during Electric. There will be relief just before and after midnight. The baby will be hot against your thighs, your stomach. It will buzz against your ribs and want to be free.

All day, in the stinking heat you lie and wait for the baby to come.

Heat Hallucination:

Your baby sister is underneath the wormwood tree. You drag her there to keep her safe from the dogs. Sometimes you kiss her face and hands. But her tiny feet, the last of her candy pink nail gloss clinging to the nails, are still yours. You put her bluish foot at your cunt sometimes, at the place where her baby sister will emerge. You want them to know each other, to connect.

Masturbation

Following fasting, you may masturbate for two hours continuously.

You may lie in the foliage.

You may come repeatedly.

You may stain your dress.

You may touch yourself and think of roses on a wedding cake.

You may cry.

You may scorch on bare knucklebones.

You may leave a static finger-trail.

You may fall into the floor.

Branding

Throw away poison comb.

Leave your fox brush wild.

Stark, hollow eyes and red, red mouth.

Lobotomy

His eyes are scalded. His eyes are burned blue.

He was on my bed. On the bed he'd killed my sister in. The soil was still packed tightly in the frame, heaped on his body. He hadn't wanted to play our last game, the game where I hit him on the head so many times until he was still. Still, not dead. And now he lay underneath the soil, his head alone raised above the dirt. He would have died, but I thrust two fingers into that filthy cavern of his mouth and scooped out the soil, scraping at his bulbous epiglottis, dead pink flesh sticking to my nails. I pushed my fingers into him again; this time he gagged and a thin string of green bile flew out. He coughed and breathed more easily.

In my pocket there was an ice pick. It was just a small thing, a little sliver of flashing metal. He hadn't seen me take it earlier, when we had gone to get the vats of acid from the kitchen.

He was the last one, the last one but for me and the baby. And the baby was months away. His eyes were blue from the acid. It scalded the jelly down to nothing, exposed the now faulty veins and nerves. Bluish juice dripped down and a sharp, hot stink rose. He was, I was, we were charged. A sizzle of electricity ran down the walls, the wiring came away in blackened peels, hot plastic oozed melts of colour down the paint—it was a room full of nausea and rot.

Rupture

The aperture slides open and red meat cracks.

Glottal valleys rise.

At this point, swallow the dark row of pins.

Blue Virgin

We went to the swimming hole. We made a daisy chain that stretched around the body of the blue virgin three times. We machined the flowers into a holy reel.

Two tears leaked on her plaster face and starred tracks ran down. When we touched the blue of her with our bare fingertips, they blackened and failed.

In the eighth month we complained that the heaviness pressed down on us, layers of dirt and matter decomposing in our guts. In the hot rooms with curtains drawn there was no release.

Coming here was cool, it was virgin blue.

Glow in the Dark Virgin

She is sad.

She is hanging from a tree, dead reels unspooled and scuttering around her body, chains around her ankles.

It is Electric, and she will be flashed repeatedly with false luminol ... until she rises, until she floats away.

The saints see her coming, watch her body shimmer on the sky.

The bloody transparencies they pull from their abdomens will cushion her great fall, her shattering delayed.

She is sad. She sees all.

Rosary Virgin

To press the screams out of her, drip the crystal beads through your fingers.

You are not invited to her distress. You must use this reel to assuage her.

1. Sorrowful

2. Agonies

3. Mysteries

4. Shadows

5. Guttings

6. Wreakings

7. Blindings

Luminol Virgin

You may use this reel to contact her directly, but do not beg to see the luminol glow.

There have been several sightings of the virgin, but none have been verified. There are many false luminol flashes, particularly near the saints. Cardiac spores have been swallowed near the grottoes to invite luminol fatality. There have been flashes across the sky at these times, but death is always instantaneous.

You may pray in any way you choose—knees on the ground, lying vitally, fucking, ripping, chest bare.

Praying is not a requirement, she will come anyway.

If you are to attend a luminol mass, you must fast, pray, purify and meditate beforehand.

Touch yourself erotically during prayer. There must be group sex throughout the blindings. Chastity belts can be removed with the shucking knife if necessary. Each pearl that rolls free must be caught and used as an offering.

SACRIFICIAL

LAWS

Offerings

FREEDOM

There is only one chance for freedom and that is to enslave the others. If you attempt this, you should write your hate on grey glass paper and bring it to the altar.

BIRTHING

This is never easy. You must find the jars of foetal matter and bring them to the altar. When you are there you must cry over the foetal matter and let the salt tenderise the meat. No one can see you do this, so it is best to go at change of shift, when there is a rush. Pull out your pearl and leave it for her.

SEX

Sex should never be attempted without appeasement. Leave a trick of bullets by her feet.

BEFORE A PAGEANT

Never speak of the pageant. Do not think of the pageant. Blur your mind with sex and colours.

CURSE

Take a sack of offcuts, preferably legs, and cure them for ten days. Bake them in the oven and roll them through the rose heap. Bake seven pattycakes into heart shapes, covered in pink icing. Leave them at the grotto. Not one crumb will remain.

Meditation

When internal lacerations break down the food source, turn to your Meditation reel.

You are allowed six sessions per calendar year, with the majority falling in Bone. It may be possible to withdraw the sixth session should your girl die within the period. Menstrual blood will be measured in the cups provided and then evaporated. Open the chest cavity with a y-incision and then palpate symmetrically. If, after six sessions, there is no solution, you may drink the luminol.

Fasting

If you die during fasting, you will be given a pageant and posthumous crown.

Before you hurt, you must fast. Nothing is to be ingested—no pattycake, no dill pickle, no girlflesh, no metallic salts and no luminol—before the work begins.

You must reduce down in size, until the bones show clear and icy beneath your skin. Your flesh must go through four stages—grease and pus will run out as the toxins release, there will be sagging as the flesh loosens beneath, bluing will occur as blood vessels tighten and strain, and finally, there will be sucking to the bone. Your skin will be slick, plumb, taut.

Internal organs become shrivelled after four weeks. The stomach will harden. Daily intravenous shots of gold will be given to maintain energy.

You will begin to feel nauseous if you smell flesh. You must stay distant from the wolf bone fires, the kitchen and the oven. You must not even enter surgery as the fluids may cause you to faint.

You may break the fast following successful completion of the hurting. Food must be reintroduced slowly, and gold shots accordingly reduced.

Waste

During Fur, when the air is dead with heaving, you may each try once for the key. The key is silver and shares a ring with trinkets from the desert; two milk teeth, plaited red hair, a fingerbone and three dried veins. The prizes click together on the ring, keeping the key safe. It can shut off the machinery, the factory, the fairground and the oven. It can set you free. Or you can cage the others. The key is deep in the bottom of the trash pile, buried in waste.

The smell is bad there because of the mounds of elephant faeces, the offcuts from the cadaver show, the rusting machine parts—all run through the crusher. The metal teeth of the apparatus are not clean, shit and fat drips down from the dark prongs, the stench compacts in the white noon. Underneath the machine lies your martyred sister, the virgin, her maggoty holes growing bigger than what remains.

Digging

This reel is sacred punishment.

Topsoil must be turned daily. Ground mulch, milled bone and fatty slough is embedded in this way. Each morning, take a sack of ground debris and walk into the desert. All human excess must be buried. If it is not possible to bury the remnants, you must scatter them in the sand. If there is any blood left, mix it through the earth with the flat edge of the spade. Dig furiously for forty minutes. Stop. Drink a portion of metallic salts. Dig furiously again for twenty minutes. Lie in the sand and use the heft of your body to close over any cracks or fissures. You may eat a fraction of the runoff to prepare you for the walk back to the factory. If you vomit, cover it in the bluest sand. If you retain the meal, return immediately.

Purification

Take off your skin to the elbow to begin this reel.

Rough hacking is effective, but for quicker results use domestic flesh stripper. Once the muscle plate is revealed, burn your number into it. Once you have been branded, take the flesh heap (if there is any remaining) and throw it down the kitchen chute.

Walk to the centre of the desert, in the direction of the sun. If more than forty paces are required to do this, you may chew on a single fingerbone. When you have consumed the bone, continue forty more paces or until you reach the spot.

When you reach the central gravesite, unpeel your breasts from their bones and lay them down. Take the iron and press the scald to your clavicle. Do not do this for more than ten seconds at a time (in order not to arouse the hunger of the saints). When you are entirely flat, you may enter the pool of holy water.

The reel will end on a miracle loop.

Shucking Knife

Use the shucking knife to splice the reel together. In this way you can bring the girls back to life and make their bodies whole. If you do not get the knack of the timing, you will make them worse—they will seem deader than before.

The shucking knife is passed down through a matriarchal line.

The shucking knife can be used to remove the pearl before or after birth.

If you experiment sexually with knife play, be careful to use rubbing alcohol on the wounds to prevent interstitial pregnancies.

Oysters can be swallowed directly from the desert pools. They should on no account be shucked clean.

Hammer

There may be some demand for the hammer. Go to the nailed-up trailer and introduce the game.

If breathing ceases or aneurysm bursts, add filters to the screaming—beige, mustard or celeriac tones can be used on the synesthesiac. Turkish Delight can be used to replace the internal organs if there is no real desire to sluice.

Mucking

Be cautious when approaching the saints. Never go without full mask and oxygen. The three implements you need for this task are the portable cylinder (which you must strap to your back), the bucket of iodine, and the spongestick.

The saints will be frightened, and will scurry to the top of their poles when they see you coming. Beware falling faeces at this point. Mildew air is green around the muck. Fill the buckets, fizz the iodine with rot. Inhale two sharp breaths of oxygen and come away.

Any flash that comes from them is false-luminol: do not turn towards it; they are charlatans.

Feeding

BEAR

Baby bear baby bear.
She has white fur and she is lonely.
Suckle her at midnight.

PATTYCAKES

The optimum grease is found inside the viscera. Remove each piece with care. When the organ slips out of the skimming, rush into a cloth sack. The surface will be slippery but tough. Take your shucking knife and slit into snowflake cadence. Make each plum lung and blue heart paper chain pretty. All the time you are doing this, grease will coat the plate and can be siphoned off. Hang up the viscera, ready for the sweet fifteen. Take the grease from the plate and mould between your palms— steady rhythmic motions will create the perfect pattycake. Ingest with acid stars and you will see the luminol flash at dawn. Leave this reel running to prevent bear death.

Reading

There is only one true reel.

This is a morning task. Once complete you may drink a portion of metallic salts and return to the assembly line. The others must be exfoliated. This reel—the one true reel—must be committed to memory twice per day. The first time will be gruelling. You will be in handstand position, paper fed roughly down your gullet until you are blue. If you lose height, poise or grace, repeat the task. Once you have committed the true reel to memory, you will be absolved. When your memory is clean of the reel, you may begin the task for the second time. This time you will be lying down. Each word must be learned rapidly and dildos applied to your sweet spot as you think.

The other reels must be rubbed with pig lard, kept clean, their spines shining with pattycake grease. Once this task has been completed, burn them with wolf bones and the saints' robes in the central furnace.

Mending

Finally, there will be luminol.

JOINTS

Joints which may suffer from corpse-weight are knees, ankles and shoulders. Beeswax cylinders must be rolled verbally until you achieve a lacquer shine. Swimming is optimum and must be practised dry for the first six months.

MACHINERY

There will be rusting machinery, metal teeth. There will be sweet sixteens, quinceañeras. There will be white dresses sprayed with blood. Pink candles, dripping wax. Christmas pattycakes full of Jesus' afterbirth. There will be nails in your palms. There will be baby bears hungry for your fall.

Bone Saint

There is nothing left of her. She sways in the wind. Her platform is a meatheap—the slough and offcut of her flagellations lie in thick layers on the wood.

The shucking knife is in her waistband. She feels every scrape of it against her bare belly. A neon thrill goes through her as metal licks flesh.

She raises her eyes to the virgin and blue light rains down. She is luminol pretty. Her scabs become a lace of glitter. The untouched pattycake, piped in yellow roses for her birthday, melts in the sun and she smiles.

Metal Saint

The first time you watch this reel, do it with a blindfold.

Slowly lift the silk from your eyes and let the sharpness come into focus. Unless you want an iron shock—in that case pin open your eyes and let it flood you.

There are one hundred precious metals in this reel. They have been slaughter-mined.

Flash Saint

This reel has been sealed in plastic and buried in the blue sand. When you open it, do it with tact—there is a gelignite sanction internally. Touch it once and the saint will appear, or you may touch it a hundred times and nothing will happen except that the flesh will burn from your fingers.

The explosives are tiny crystals of light—afterbirth, coeliac and winedark.

Once you release the saint from this reel he will be thick upon you. He will mist you in ghoul smoke. He will suck.

If you see his face, you are ended. It is the face of the bad man.

Jewel Saint

If you use the oven terminally, you become a jewel saint.

This reel is a compilation of all the gassings. The oven is wiped clean, silver. Stop motion poisons leak from it.

If you look deep into the mouth of the oven, you can see death, the apocalypse, violence.

You can be in the metal tunnel.

Throw the following items into the flames: water, glitter, foil, food.

The flames will change colour and sputter.

Blow out the flames on your sweet sixteen and lie down.

Bone

This season is the hardest. Never insert this reel until ready for blunt trauma.

The only way to exist in Bone is to find a window or a view. We lie mute and seasick, watching the sky turn grey, black.

Our bodies roll through bronze shavings, through tarpaper.

Fur

This is the season for hunting. There are foxes, squirrels, deer and baby bears.

Take your shucking knife up close to them while they are sleeping and slide it under their sleek pelts.

You can spear them from a distance.

You can burn them out of their holes, caves and clearings.

Wrestle them to the ground.

You can hatefuck them.

Wear them at Christmas.

You can lie on their soft, brown pelts and make generic love.

Dry

Your biggest problem will be loss of mineral salts. Remedy this by applying in conjunction with the Holy Water reel.

You will be awake all night thinking about falling.

You will have a black headache that spreads right through with needlepoints of pain.

Your eye sockets are filled with gritty greyish putty, bandaged.

Your task is to count your breaths as you spin out the hours.

If you wish (for relief), you may scream.

Electric

Napalm, sulphur and asbestos storms hit in Electric.
There is no shelter.

Roseheap

During Roseheap you will be tired all the time.

Turn this reel on only if you are prepared to face your end.

The night is bad but the day is worse. Sunlight will be horror, a bad thing. The new day brings dogs with teeth. Patch the walls of the factory with runoff. Slough yourselves in stinks. The scent of nutmeg will creep from your apron. Your bare head will leak coconut oil.

You will work the fair by night, dresses soaked with red diesel from the carnival, the big dipper shuddering on its tracks and needing more fuel. By day keep the reels clean, pig lard rubbed along the spines, covers of thin bone.

THE DEAD RETURN

End

It was a long way out to the edge of the desert, to where the cherry wine factory girls made out with bad men.

The dogs were hungry as usual when we prepared for the chase. Six white hounds, purebred and eager. We lay on the ground beside them, in the enclosure where they slept. We had raw meat in our pockets—elephant hide or fish guts or maybe girl parts we couldn't boil down. We passed the meat from our mouths to theirs, chewing it slowly, tenderising, until it was soft enough for them to digest. Used to our scent and keen for treats, the dogs rolled over when we came near, their grey underbellies exposed. We stroked their velvet pelts gently, until each hair was on end in a field of static. Only then, when the beasts were quivering under our touch, did we drop food into their mouths. Yelping, the dogs rolled back on to their feet, scenting blood, hungry for the chase.

We liked to charge into the black rocks. It was a beautiful ride out—the copper sky burned gold in the heat and the rocks sent out sparks of black light. Our hands were velvet from the chase. Our toes and fingers were indistinct, padded with hard calluses worn smooth. We glided through the sand—the sky bent lower to the ground leaking oily warmth. Our eyes stung with salt.

The reel ends in a bad way. We are in the grip of something terrible, a hallucination. We crawl—burning sand sticking to the leather on our knees, water from our canteens leaking and hissing on the desert ground. As it vanishes, we begin to laugh ... a low sound swallowed in the soupy sky.

Lying dazed on our backs, we see the desert all at once. Black light zinging from the rocks, the bluish sand glittering. Blood dripping from our broken necks, we let out a high whistle that only the hounds understand. We slip under then, deep under, as noon melts the sky.

Psychic

We had the last séance.

We dressed in rags and tatters, smeared and stinking ballgowns. We were looped with fairy lights and wore plastic crowns.

The girls called out to me, and the saints and virgins hummed through. A snowy sludge of sound that rang ice into the room.

L U M I N O L

and

M U R D E R

and

F A C T O R Y

were the words they spelled out.

Revelation

Oxidation of luminol is attended by a striking emission of blue-green light. An alkaline solution of the compound is allowed to react with a mixture of hydrogen peroxide and potassium ferricyanide. The dianion (5) is oxidized to the triplet excited state (two unpaired electrons of like spin) (6) of the amino phthalate ion (Scheme 2). This slowly undergoes intersystem crossing to the singlet excited state (two unpaired electrons of opposite spin) (7), which decays to the ground state ion (8) with the emission of one quantum of light (a photon) per molecule.